I0761951

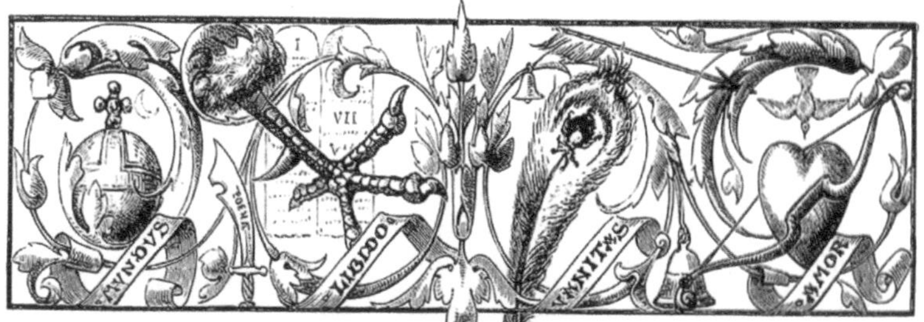
MVNDVS
LIBIDO
AMOR

TERRA

"IF YOU GAZE LONG ENOUGH
INTO AN ABYSS, THE ABYSS
WILL GAZE BACK INTO YOU"
(Friedrich Nietzsche)

COELVM

ANIMA
MALVM
MORS
STVLTITIA

LEGATUS BOOKS:

ALEISTER CROWLEY

THE TESTAMENT OF MAGDALEN BLAIR

LEGATUS

I Edition: May 2020
ISBN 978-1-8380473-0-6

Legatus LTD - Scotland

Editor:
Giancarlo D'Anello

Designer:
Natalia Strazzeri

Proofreader:
Euclides Cantidiano

www.editoralegatus.com

To my mother

THE TESTAMENT OF MAGDALEN BLAIR

PART I

I

In my third term at Newnham I was already Professor Blair's favourite pupil. Later, he wasted a great deal of time praising my slight figure and my piquant face, with its big round grey eyes and their long black lashes; but the first attraction was my singular gift. Few men, and, I believe, no other women, could approach me in one of the most priceless qualifications for scientific study, the faculty of apprehending minute differences. My memory was poor, extraordinarily so; I had the utmost trouble to enter Cambridge at all. But I could adjust a micrometer better than either students or professor, and read a vernier with an accuracy to which none of them could even aspire. To this I added a faculty of subconscious calculation which was really uncanny. If I were engaged in keeping a solution between (say) 70 Degree and 80 Degrees I had no need to watch the thermometer. Automatically I became aware that the mercury was close to the limit, and would go over from my other work and adjust it[1] without a thought.

More remarkable still, if any object were placed on my bench without my knowledge and then removed, I could, if asked within a few minutes, describe the object roughly, especially distinguishing the shape of its base and the degree of its opacity to heat and light. From these data I could make a pretty good guess at what the object was.

***1.** Ed.: The Bunsen burner is an instrument used in chemistry. It takes its name from Robert Wilhelm Bunsen, a 19th century German physicist.*

This faculty of mine was repeatedly tested, and always with success.Extreme sensitiveness to minute degrees of heat was its obvious cause.

I was also a singularly good thought-reader, even at this time. The other girls feared me absolutely. They need not have done so; I had neither ambition nor energy to make use of any of my powers. Even now, when I bring to mankind this message of a doom so appalling that at the age of twenty-four I am a shrivelled, blasted, withered wreck, I am supremely weary, supremely indifferent.

I have the heart of a child and the consciousness of Satan, the lethargy of I know not what disease; and yet, thank — oh! there can be no God! — the resolution to warn mankind to follow my example, and then to explode a dynamite cartridge in my mouth.

II

In my third year at Newnham I spend four hours of every day at Professor Blair's house. All other work was neglected, gone through mechanically, if at all. This came about gradually, as the result of an accident.

The chemical laboratory has two rooms, one small and capable of being darkened. On this occasion (the May term of my second year) this room was in use. It was the first week of June, and extremely fine. The door was shut. Within was a girl, alone, experimenting with the galvanometer.

I was absorbed in my own work. Quite without warning I looked up. "Quick!" said I, "Gladys is going to faint." Every one in the room stared at me. I took a dozen steps towards the door, when the fall of a heavy body sent the laboratory into hysterics.

It was only the heat and confined atmosphere, and Gladys should not have come to work that day at all, but she was easily revived, and then the demonstrator acquiesced in the anarchy that followed. "How did she know?" was the universal query; for that I knew was evident. Ada Brown *("Athanasia contra mundum")*[2] pooh-poohed the whole affair; Margaret Letchmere thought I must have heard something, perhaps a cry inaudible to the others, owing to their occupied attention; Doris Leslie spoke of second sight, and Amy Gore of "Sympathy." All the theories, taken together, went round the clock of conjecture. Professor Blair came in at the most excited part of the discussion, calmed the room in two minutes, elicited the

---

2. *Ed.: Wrong spelling of Athanasius, a 4th century bishop of Alexandria who stated: "Even if I must be against the world, I will persist in my struggle".*

facts in five, and took me off to dine with him. "I believe it's this human thermopile affair of yours," he said. "Do you mind if we try a few parlour tricks after dinner?" His aunt, who kept house for him,protested in vain, and was appointed Grand Superintendent in Ordinary of my five senses.

My hearing was first tested, and found normal, or thereabouts. I was then blindfolded, and the aunt (by excess of precaution) stationed between me and the Professor. I found that I could describe even small movements that he made, so long as he was between me and the western window, not at all when he moved round to the other quarters. This is in conformity with the "Thermopile" theory; it was contradicted completely on other occasions. The results (in short) were very remarkable and very puzzling; we wasted two precious hours in futile theorizing. In the event the aunt (cowed by a formidable frown) invited me to spend the Long Vacation in Cornwall.

During these months the Professor and I assiduously worked to discover exactly the nature and limit of my powers. The result, in a sense, was "nil."For one thing, these powers kept on "breaking out in a new place." I seemed to do all I did by perception of minute differences; but then it seemed as if I had all sorts of different apparatus. "One down, t'other come on [3]," said Professor Blair.

Those who have never made scientific experiments cannot conceive how numerous and subtle are the sources of error, even in the simplest matters. In so obscure and novel a field of research no result is trustworthy until it has been verified a thousand times. In our field we discovered no constants, all variables.

Although we had hundreds of facts any one of which seemed capable of overthrowing all accepted theories of the means of communication between mind and mind, we had nothing,

---

3. *Ed.: Reference to one of the principles attributed to Hermes Trismegistus, who wrote that "Everything flows out and in; everything has its tides; all things rise and fall; the pendulum swing manifests in everything; the measure of the swing to the right, is the measure of the swing to the left; rhythm compensates".*

absolutely nothing, which we could use as the basis of a new theory.

It is naturally impossible to give even an outline of the course of our research. Twenty-eight closely written notebooks referring to this first period are at the disposal of my executors.

les Catacombes

III

In the middle of the day, in my third year, my father was dangerously ill. I bicycled over to Peterborough at once, never thinking of my work. (My father is a canon of Peterborough Cathedral.) On the third day I received a telegram from Professor Blair, "Will you be my wife?" I had never realized myself as a woman, or him as a man, till that moment, and in that moment I knew that I loved him and had always loved him. It was a case of what one might call "Love at first absence." My father recovered rapidly; I returned to Cambridge; we were married during the May week[4] , and

---

4. *Ed.: May Week is the term that indicates the end of the academic year in Cambridge.*

went immediately to Switzerland. I beg to be spared any recital of so sacred a period of my life: but I must record one fact.

We were sitting in a garden by Lago Maggiore after a delightful tramp from Chamounix over the Col du Geant to Courmayeur, and thence to Aosta, and so by degrees to Pallanza. Arthur rose, apparently struck by some idea, and began to walk up and down the terrace. "I was quite suddenly impelled to turn my head to assure myself of his presence."

This may seem nothing to you who read, unless you have true imagination. But think of yourself talking to a friend in full light, and suddenly leaning forward to touch him. "Arthur!" I cried, "Arthur!"

The distress in my tone brought him running to my side. "What is it, Magdalen?" he cried, anxiety in every word.

I closed my eyes. "Make gestures!" said I. (He was directly between me and the sun.)

He obeyed, wondering.

"You are - your are" - I stammered -"no! I don't know what you are doing. I am blind!"

He sawed his arm up and down. Useless; I had become absolutely insensitive. We repeated a dozen experiments that night. All failed.

We concealed our disappointment, and it did not cloud our love. The sympathy between us grew even subtler and stronger, but only as it grows between all men and women who love with their whole hearts, and love unselfishly.

IV

We returned to Cambridge in October, and Arthur threw himself vigorously into the new year's work. Then I fell ill, and the hope we had indulged was disappointed. Worse, the course of the illness revealed a condition which demanded the most complete series of operations which a woman can endure. Not only the past hope, but all future hope, was annihilated.

It was during my convalescence that the most remarkable incident of my life took place.

I was in great pain one afternoon, and wished to see the doctor. The nurse went to the study to telephone for him.

"Nurse!" I said, as she returned, "don't lie to me. He's not gone to Royston; he's got cancer, and is too upset to come."

"Whatever next?" said the nurse. "It's right he can't come, and I was going to tell you he had gone to Royston; but I never heard nothing about no cancer."

This was true; she had not been told. But the next morning we heard that my "intuition" was correct.

As soon as I was well enough, we began our experiments again. My powers had returned, and in triple force.

Arthur explained my "intuition" as follows: "The doctor (when you last saw him) did not know consciously that he had cancer; but subconsciously Nature gave warning. You read this subconsciously, and it sprang into your consciousness when you read on the nurse's face that he was ill."

This, farfetched as it may seem, at least avoids the shallow theories about "telepathy."

From this time my powers constantly increased. I could read my husband's thoughts from imperceptible movements of his face as easily as a trained deaf-mute can sometimes read the speech of a distant man from the movements of his lips.

Gradually as we worked, day by day, I found my grasp of detail ever fuller. It is not only that I could read emotions; I could tell whether he was thinking 3465822 or 3456822. In the year following my illness we made 436 experiments of this kind, each extending over several hours; in all 9363, with only 122 failures, and these all, without exception, partial.

The year following, our experiments were extended to a reading of his dreams. In this I proved equally successful. My practice was to leave the room before he woke, write down the dream that he had dreamt, and await him at the breakfast-table, where he would compare his record with mine.

Invariably they were identical, with this exception, that my record was always much fuller than his. He would nearly always, however, purport to remember the details supplied by me; but this detail has (I think) no real scientific value.

But what does it all matter, when I think of the horror impending?

V

That my only means of discovering Arthur's thought was by muscle-reading became more than doubtful during the third year of our marriage. We practised "telepahty" unashamed. We excluded the "muscle-reader" and the "super-auditor" and the "human thermopile" by elaborate precautions; yet still I was able to read every thought of his mind. On our holiday in North Wales at Easter one year we separated for a week, at the end of that week he to be on the leeward, I on the windward side of Tryfan, at an appointed hour, he there to open and read to himself a sealed packet given him by "some stranger met at Pen-y-Pass during the week."

The experiment was entirely successful; I reproduced every word of the document. If the "telepathy" is to be vitiated, it is on the theory that I had previously met the "stranger" and read from him what he would write in such circumstances! Surely direct communication of mind with mind is an easier theory!

Had I known in what all this was to culminate, I suppose I should have gone mad. Thrice fortunate that I can warn humanity of what awaits each one. The greatest benefactor of his race will be he who discovers and explosive indefinitely swifter and more devastating than dynamite. If I could only trust myself to prepare Chloride of Nitrogen in sufficient quantity. …

VI

Arthur became listless and indifferent. The perfection of love that had been our marriage failed without warning, and yet by imperceptible gradations.

My awakening to the fact was, however, altogether sudden. It was one summer evening; we were paddling on the Cam. One of Arthur's pupils, also in a Canadian canoe, challenged us to race. At Magdalen Bridge we were a length ahead - suddenly I heard my husband's thought. It was the most hideous and horrible laugh that it is possible to conceive. No devil could laugh so. I screamed, and dropped my paddle. Both the men thought me ill. I assured myself that it was not the laugh of some townee on the bridge, distorted by my over-sensitive organization. I said no more; Arthur looked grave. At night he asked abruptly after a long period of brooding, "Was that my thought?" I could only stammer that I did not know. Incidentally he complained of fatigue, and the listlessness, which before had seemed nothing to me, assumed a ghastly shape. There was something in him that was not he! The indifference had appeared transitory; I now became aware of it as constant and increasing. I was at this time twenty-three years old. You wonder that I write with such serious attitude of mind. I sometimes think that I have never had any thoughts of my own; that I have always been reading the thoughts of another, or perhaps of Nature. I seem only to have been a woman in those first few months of marriage.

VII

The six months following held for me nothing out of the ordinary, save that six or seven times I had dreams, vivid and terrible. Arthur had no share in these; yet I knew, I cannot say how, that they were his dreams and not mine; or rather that they were in his subconscious waking self, for one occurred in the afternoon, when he was out shooting, and not in the least asleep.

The last of them occurred towards the end of the October term. He was lecturing as usual, I was at home, lethargic after a too heavy breakfast following a wakeful night. I saw suddenly a picture of the lecture-room, enormously greater than in reality, so that it filled all space; and in the rostrum, bulging over it in all directions, was a vast, deadly pale devil with a face which was a blasphemy on Arthur's. The evil joy of it was indescribable. So wan and bloated, its lips so loose and bloodless; fold after fold of its belly flopping over the rostrum and pushing the students out of the hall, it leered unspeakably. Then dribbled from its mouth these words: "Ladies and gentlemen, the course is finished. You may go home." I cannot hope even to suggest the wickedness and filth of these simple expressions. Then, raising its voice to a grating scream, it yelled: "White of egg! White of egg! White of egg!" again and again for twenty minutes.

The effect on me was shocking. It was as if I had a vision of Hell.

Arthur found me in a very hysterical condition, but soon soothed me. "Do you know," he said at dinner, "I believe I have got a devilish bad chill?"

It was the first time I had known him to complain of his health. In six years he had not had as much as a headache.

I told him my "dream" when we were in bed, and he seemed unusually grave, as if he understood where I had failed in its interpretation. In the morning he was feverish; I made him stay in bed and sent for the doctor. The same afternoon I learnt that Arthur was seriously ill, had been ill, indeed, for months. The doctor called it Bright's[5] disease.

---

5. *Ed.: An old term that used to indicate what we know today as chronic renal failure. It takes its name in honor of the doctor Richard Bright.*

VIII

I said "the last of the dreams." For the next year we travelled, and tried various treatments. My powers remained excellent, but I received none of the subconscious horrors. With few fluctuations, he grew steadily worse; daily he became more listless, more indifferent, more depressed. Our experiments were necessarily curtailed. Only one problem exercised him, the problem of his personality. He began to wonder "who he was." I do not mean that he suffered from delusions. I mean that the problem of the true Ego took hold of his imagination. One perfect summer night at Contrexeville he was feeling much better; the symptoms had (temporarily) disappeared almost entirely under the treatment of a very skilful doctor at that Spa, a Dr. Barbezieux, a most kind and thoughtful man.

"I am going to try," said Arthur, "to penetrate myself. Am I an animal, and is the world without a purpose? Or am I a soul in a body? Or am I, one and indivisible in some incredible sense, a spark of the infinite light of God? I am going to think inwards: I shall possibly go into some form of trance, unintelligible to myself. You may be able to interpret it."

The experiment had lasted about half an hour when he sat up gasping with effort.

"I have seen nothing, heard nothing," I said. "Not one thought has passed from you to me."

But at that very moment what had been in his mind flashed into mine.

"It is a blind abyss," I told him, "and there hangs in it a vulture vaster than the whole starry system."

"Yes," he said, "that was it. But that was not all. I could not get beyond it. I shall try again."He tried. Again I was cut off from his thought, although his face was twitching so that one might have said that any one might read his mind.

"I have been looking in the wrong place," said he suddenly, but very quietly and without moving. "The thing I want lies at the base of the spine[6]."

This time I saw. In a blue heaven was coiled an infinite snake of gold and green, with four eyes of fire, black fire and red, that darted rays in every direction; held within its coils was a great multitude of laughing children. And even as I looked, all this was blotted out. Crawling rivers of blood spread over the heaven, of blood purulent with nameless forms — mangy dogs with their bowels dragging behind them; creatures half elephant, half beetle; things that were but a ghastly bloodshot eye, set about with leathery tentacles; women whose skins heaved and bubbled like boiling sulphur, giving off clouds that condensed into a thousand other shapes, more hideous than their mother; these were the least of the denizens of these hateful

---

6. *Ed.: Reference to Kundalini, a divine energy that Hindus believed that is located at the base of the spine. The snake is showed as a symbolic image of the Kundalini, which was understood as a potent force that is normally found at rest.*

rivers. The most were things impossible to name or to describe.

I was brought back from the vision by the stertorous and strangling breath of Arthur, who had been seized with a convulsion.

From this he never really rallied. The dim sight grew dimmer, the speech slower and thicker, the headaches more persistent and acute.

Torpor succeeded to his old splendid energy and activity; his days became continual lethargy ever deepening towards coma. Convulsions now and then alarmed me for his immediate danger.

Sometimes his breath came hard and hissing like a snake in anger; towards the end it assumed the Cheyne-Stokes[7] type in bursts of ever-increasing duration and severity.

In all this, however, he was still himself; the horror that was and yet was not himself did not peer from behind the veil

"So long as I am consciously myself," he said in one of his rare fits of brightness, "I can communicate to you what I am consciously thinking; as soon as this conscious ego is absor-

---

7. Ed.: It is a pathological breathing that alternates between apnea and deep breathing.

bed, you get the subconscious thought which I fear - oh how I fear! - is the greater and truer part of me. You have brought unguessed explanations from the world of sleep; you are the one woman in the world - perhaps there may never be another - who has such an opportunity to study the phenomena of death."

He charged me earnestly to suppress my grief, to concentrate wholly on the thoughts that passed through his mind when he could no longer express them, and also on those of his subconsciousness when coma inhibited consciousness.

It is this experiment that I now force myself to narrate. The prologue has been long; it has been necessary to put the facts before mankind in a simple way so that they may seize the opportunity of the proper kind of suicide. I beg my readers most earnestly not to doubt my statements: the notes of our experiments, left in my will to the greatest thinker now living, Professor von Buhle, will make clear the truth of my relation, and the great and terrible necessity of immediate, drastic, action.

PART II

I

he stunning physical fact of my husband's illness was the immense prostration. So strong a body, as too often the convulsions gave proof; such inertia with it! He would lie all day like a log; then without warning or apparent cause the convulsions would begin. Arthur's steady scientific brain stood it well; it was only two days before his death that delirium began. I was not with him; worn out as I was, and yet utterly unable to sleep, the doctor had insisted on my taking a long motor drive. In the fresh air I slumbered. I awoke to hear an unfamiliar voice saying in my ear, "Now for the fun of the fair!" There was no one there. Quick on its heels followed my husband's voice as I had long since known and loved it, clear, strong, resonant, measured: "Get this down right; it is very important. I am passing into the power of the subconsciousness. I may not be able to speak to you again. But I am here; I am not to be touched by all that I may suffer; I can always think; you can always read my –" The voice broke off sharply to inquire, "But will it ever end?" as if some one had spoken to it. And then I heard the laugh. The laugh that I had heard by Magdalen Bridge was heavenly music beside that! The face of Calvin (even) as he gloated over the burning of Servetus[8] would have turned

---

8. Ed.: Reference to Miguel Servet, a Renaissance theologian and humanist who, after being condemned as a heretic by the French authorities, was burned alive. John Calvin was one of the men who denounced him.

pitiful had he heard it, so perfectly did it express quintessence of damnation.

Now then my husband's thought seemed to have changed places with the other. It was below, within, withdrawn. I said to myself, "He is dead!" Then came Arthur's thought, "I had better pretend to be mad. It will save her, perhaps; and it will be a change. I shall pretend I have killed her with an axe. Damn it! I hope she is not listening" I was now thoroughly awake, and told the drive to get home quickly. "I hope she is killed in the motor; I hope she is smashed into a million pieces. O God! hear my one prayer! let an Anarchist throw a bomb and smash Magdalen into a million pieces! especially the brain! and the brain first. O God! my first and last prayer: smash Magdalen into a million pieces!"

The horror of this thought was my conviction - then and now - that it represented perfect sanity and coherence of thought. For I dreaded utterly to think what such words might imply.

At the door of the sick-room I was met by the male nurse, who asked me not to enter. Uncontrollably, I asked, "Is he dead?" and though Arthur lay absolutely senseless on the bed I read the answering thought "Dead!" silently pronounced in such tones of mockery, horror, cynicism and despair as I never thought to hear. There was a something or somebody who suffered infinitely, and yet who gloated infinitely upon that very suffering. And that something was a veil between me and Arthur.

The hissing breath recommenced; Arthur seem to be trying to express himself - the self I knew. He managed to articulate feebly, "Is that the police? Let me get out of the house! The police are coming for me. I killed Magdalen with an axe." The symptoms of delirium began to appear. "I killed Magdalen" he muttered a dozen times, than changing to "Magdalen with" again and again; the voice low, slow, thick, yet reiterated. Then suddenly, quite clear and loud, attempting to rise in the bed: "I smashed Magdalen into a million pieces with an axe." After a moment's pause: "a million is not very many now-a-days." From this - which I now see to have been the speech of a sane Arthur - he dropped again into delirium. "A million pieces," "a cool million," "a million million

million million million million" and so on: then abruptly: "Fanny's dog's dead."

I cannot explain the last sentence to my readers; I may, however, remark that it meant everything to me. I burst into tears. At that moment I caught Arthur's thought, "You ought to be busy with the note-book, not crying." I resolutely dried my eyes, took courage, and began to write.

II

The doctor came in at this moment and begged me to go and rest. "You are only distressing yourself, Mrs. Blair," he said; "and needlessly, for he is absolutely unconscious and suffers nothing." A pause. "My God! why do you look at me like that?" he exclaimed, frightened out of his wits. I think my face had caught something of that devil's, something of that sneer, that loathing, that mire of contempt and stark despair.

I sank back into myself, ashamed already that mere knowledge - and such mean vile knowledge - should so puff one up with hideous pride. No wonder Satan fell! I began to understand all the old legends, and far more –

I told Doctor Kershaw that I was carrying out Arthur's last wishes. He raised no further opposition; but I saw him sign to the male nurse to keep an eye on me.

The sick man's finger beckoned us. He could not speak; he traced circles on the counterpane. The doctor (with characteristic intelligence) having counted the circles, nodded; and said: "Yes, it is nearly seven o'clock. Time for your medicine, eh?"

"No," I explained, "he means that he is in the seventh circle of Dante's Hell."

At that instant he entered on a period of noisy delirium. Wild and prolonged howls burst from his throat; he was being chewed unceasingly by "Dis"; each howl signalled the meeting of the monster's teeth. I explained this to the doctor. "No," said he, "he is perfectly unconscious."

"Well," said I, "he will howl about eighty times more.

Doctor Kershaw looked at me curiously, but began to count.

My calculation was correct.

He turned to me, "Are you a woman?"

"No," said I, "I am my husband's colleague."

"I think it is suggestion. You have hypnotized him?"

"Never: but I can read his thoughts."

"Yes, I remember now; I read a very remarkable paper in "Mind" two years ago."

"That was child's play. But let me go on with my work."

He gave some final instructions to the nurse, and went out.

The suffering of Arthur was at this time unspeakable. Chewed as he was into mere pulp that passed over the tongue of "Dis," each bleeding fragment kept its own identity and his. The papillae of the tongue were serpents, and each one gnashed its poisoned teeth upon that fodder.

And yet, though the sensorium of Arthur was absolutely unimpaired, indeed hyperaesthetic, his consciousness of pain seemed to depend upon the opening of the mouth. As it closed in mastication, oblivion fell upon him like a thunderbolt. A merciful oblivion? Oh! what a master stroke of cruelty! Again and again he woke from nothing to a hell of agony, of pure ecstasy of agony, until he understood that this would continue for all his life; the alternation was but systole and diastole, the throb of his envenomed pulse, the reflection in consciousness of his blood-beat. I became conscious of his intense longing for death to end the torture.

The blood circulated ever slower and more painfully; I could feel him hoping for the end.

This dreadful rose-dawn suddenly greyed and sickened with doubt. Hope sank to its nadir[9]; fear rose like a dragon, with leaden wings. Suppose, thought he, that after all death does not end me!

I cannot express this conception. It is not that the heart sank, it had nowhither to sink; it knew itself immortal, and immortal in a realm of unimagined pain and terror, unlighted by one glimpse of any other light than that pale glare of hate and of pestilence. This thought took shape in these words:

---

9. *Ed.: In astronomy and geography, nadir is the bottom point of the celestial sphere, from the perspective of an observer on the planet's surface. Here, Crowley uses the term with esoteric connotations.*

AM THAT I AM

One cannot say that the blasphemy added to the horror; rather it was the essence of the horror. It was the gnashing of the teeth of a damned soul.

III

The demon-shape, which I now clearly recognized as that which had figured in my last "dream" at Cambridge, seemed to gulp. At that instant a convulsion shook the dying man and a coughing eructation took the "demon." Instantly the whole theory dawned on me, that this "demon" was an imaginary personification of the disease. Now at once I understood demonology, from Bodin and Weirus[10] to the moderns, without a flaw. But was it imaginary or was it real? Real enough to swallow up the "sane" thought!

10. *Ed.: Jean Bodin and Johann Weyer - Crowley wrote his surname as Weirus, perhaps trying to emulate its Latin form, which would correctly be Wierus - were famous demonologists of the sixteenth century.*

At that instant the old Arthur reappeared. "I am not the monster! I am Arthur Blair, of Fettes and Trinity. I have passed through a paroxysm."

The sick man stirred feebly. A portion of his brain had shaken off the poison for the moment, and was working furiously against time.

"I am going to die.

"The consolation of death is Religion.

"There is no use for Religion in life.

"How many atheists have I not known sign the articles the sake of fellowships and livings! Religion in life is either an amusement and a soporific or a sham and a swindle.

"I was brought up a Presbyterian

"How easily I drifted into the English Church!

"And now where is God?

"Where is the Lamb of God?

"Where is the Saviour?

"Where is the Comforter?

"Why was I not saved from that devil?

"Is he going to eat me again? To absorb me into him? O fate inconceivably hideous! It is quite clear to me - I hope you've got it down, Magdalen! - that the demon is made of all those that have died of Bright's disease. There must be different ones for each disease. I thought I once caught sight of a coughing bog of bloody slime.

"Let me pray."

A frenzied appeal to the Creator followed. Sincere as it was, it would read like irreverence in print.

And then there came the cold-drawn horror of stark blasphemy against this God - who would not answer.

Followed the bleak black agony of the conviction - the absolute certitude - "There is no God!" combined with a wave of frenzied wrath against the people who had so glibly assured him that there was, an almost maniac hope that they would suffer more than he, if it were possible.

(Poor Arthur! He had not yet brushed the bloom off Suffering's grape; he was to drink its fiercest distillation to the dregs.)

"No!" thought he, "perhaps I lack their 'faith.'

"Perhaps if I could really persuade myself

of God and Christ - Perhaps if I could deceive myself, could make believe –"

Such a thought is to surrender one's honesty, to abdicate one's reason. It marked the final futile struggle of his will. The demon caught and crunched him, and the noisy delirium began anew.

My flesh and blood rebelled. Taken with a deathly vomit, I rushed from the room, and resolutely, for a whole hour, diverted my sensorium from thought. I had always found that the slightest trace of tobacco smoke in a room greatly disturbed my power. On this occasion I puffed cigarette after cigarette with excellent effect. I knew nothing of what had been going on.

OCEAN
AMERICA
INDIAN
DEATHS DANCE

IV

Arthur, stung by the venomous chyle, was tossing in that vast arched belly, which resembled the dome of hell, churned in its bubbling slime. I felt that he was not only disintegrated mechanically, but chemically, that his being was loosened more and more into its parts, that these were being absorbed into new and hateful things, but that (worst of all) Arthur stood immune from all, behind it, unimpaired, memory and reason ever more acute as ever new and ghastlier experience informed them. It seemed to me as if some mystic state were super-added to the torment; for while he was not, emphatically not, this tortured mass of consciousness, yet that was he. There are always at least two of us! The one who feels and the one who knows are not radically one person. This double personality is enormously accentuated at death.

Another point was that the time-sense, which with men is usually so reliable - especially in my own case - was decidedly deranged, if not abrogated altogether.

We all judge of the lapse of time in relation to our daily habits or some similar standard. The conviction of immortality must naturally destroy all values for this sense. If I am immortal, what is the difference between a long time and a short time? A thousand years and a day are obviously the same thing from the point of view of "for ever."

There is a subconscious clock in us, a clock wound up by the experience of the race to go for seventy years or so. Five minutes is a very long time to us if we are waiting for an omnibus, an age if we are waiting for a lover, nothing at all if we are pleasantly engaged or sleeping[11].

---

11. *N.f.A.: It is one of the greatest cruelties of nature that all painful or depressing emotions seem to lengthen time; pleasant thoughts and exalted moods make time fly. Thus, in summing up a life from an outside standpoint, it would seem that, supposing pleasure and pain to have occupied equal periods, the impression would be that pain was enormously greater than pleasure. This may be controverted. Virgil writes: "Forsitan haec olim meminisse juvabit," and there is at least one modern writer thoroughly conversant with pessimism who is very optimistic. But the new facts which I here submit overthrow the whole argument; they cast a sword of infinite weight on that petty trembling scale.*

We think of seven years as a long time in connection with penal servitude; as a negligibly small period in dealing with geology.

But, given immortality, the age of the stellar system itself is nothing.

This conviction had not fully impregnated the consciousness of Arthur; it hung over him like a threat, while the intensification of that consciousness, its liberation from the sense of time natural to life, caused each act of the demon to appear of vast duration, although the intervals between the howls of the body on the bed were very short. Each pang of torture or suspense was born, rose to its crest, and died to be reborn again through what seemed countless aeons.

Still more was this the case in the process of his assimilation by the "demon." The coma of the dying man was a phenomenon altogether out of Time. The conditions of "digestion" were new to Arthur, he had no reason to suppose, no data from which to calculate the distance of, an end.

It is impossible to do more than sketch this process; as he was absorbed, so did his consciousness expand into that of the "demon"; he became one with all its hunger and corruption. Yet always did he suffer as himself in his own person the tearing asunder of his finest molecules; and this was confirmed by a most filthy humiliation of that part of him that was rejected.

I shall not attempt to describe the final process; suffice it that the demoniac consciousness drew away; he was but the excrement of the demon, and as that excrement he was flung filthily further into the abyss of blackness and of night whose name is death.

I rose with ashen cheeks. I stammered: "He is dead." The male nurse bent over the body. "Yes!" he echoed, "he is dead." And it seemed as if the whole Universe gathered itself into one ghastly laugh of hate and horror, "Dead!"

h.D.

V

I resumed my seat. I felt that I must know that all was well, that death had ended all. Woe to humanity! The consciousness of Arthur was more alive than ever. It was the black fear of falling, a dumb ecstasy of changeless fear. There were no waves upon that sea of shame, no troubling of those accursed waters by any thought. There was no hope of any ground to that abyss, no thought that it might stop. So tireless was that fall that even acceleration was absent; it was constant and level as the fall of a star. There was not even a feeling of pace; infinitely fast as it must be, judging from the peculiar dread which it inspired, it was yet infinitely slow, having regard to the infinitude of the abyss.

I took measures not to be disturbed by the duties that men - oh how foolishly! - pay to the dead: and I took refuge in a cigarette.

It was now for the first time, strangely enough, that I began to consider the possibility of helping him.

I analysed the position. It must be his thought, or I could not read it. I had no reason to conjecture that any other thoughts could reach me. He must be alive in the true sense of the word; it was he and not another that was the prey of this fear ineffable. Of this fear it was evident that there must be a physical basis in the constitution of his brain and body. All the other phenomena had been shown to correspond exactly with a physical condition; it was the reflection in a consciousness from which human limitation had fallen away of things actually taking place in the body.

It was a false interpretation perhaps; but it was his interpretation; and it was that which caused suffering so beyond all that poets have ever dreamt of the infernal.

I am ashamed to say that my first thought was of the Catholic Church and its masses for the repose of the dead. I went to the Cathedral, revolving as I went all that had ever been said - the superstitions of a hundred savage tribes. At bottom I could find no difference between their barbarous rites and those of Christianity.

However that might be, I was baffled. The priests refused to pray for the soul of a heretic.

I hurried back to the house, resumed my vigil. There was no change, except a deepening of the fear, an intensification of the loneliness, a more utter absorption in the shame. I could but hope that in the ultimate stagnation of all vital forces, death would become final, hell merged into annihilation.

This started a train of thought which ended in a determination to hasten the process. I thought of blowing out the brains, remembered that I had no means of doing so. I thought of freezing the body, imagined a story for the nurse, reflected that no cold could excite in his soul aught icier than that illimitable void of black.

I thought of telling the doctor that he had wished to bequeath his body to the surgeons, that he had been afraid of being buried alive, anything that might induce him to remove the brain. At that moment I looked into the mirror, I saw that I must not speak. My hair was white, my face drawn, my eyes wild and bloodshot.

In utter helplessness and misery I flung myself on the couch in the study, and puffed greedily at cigarettes. The relief was so immense that my sense of loyalty and duty had a hard fight to get me to resume the task. The mingling of horror, curiosity, and excitement must have aided.

I threw away my fifth cigarette, and returned to the death chamber.

VI

Before I had sat at the table ten minutes a change burst out with startling suddenness. At one point in the void the blackness gathered, concentrated, sprang into an evil flame that gushed aimlessly forth from nowhere to nowhere.

This was accompanied by the most noxious stench.

It was gone before I could realize it. As lightning precedes thunder, it was followed by a hideous clamour that I can only describe as the cry of a machine in pain.

This recurred constantly for an hour and five minutes, then ceased as suddenly as itbegan. Arthur still fell.

It was succeeded after the lapse of five hours by another paroxysm of the same kind, but fiercer and more continuous. Another silence followed, age upon age of fear and loneliness and shame.

About midnight there appeared a grey ocean of bowels below the falling soul. This ocean seemed to be limitless. It fell headlong into it, and the splash awakened it to a new consciousness of things.

This sea, though infinitely cold, was boiling like tubercles. Itself a more or less homogeneous slime, the stench of which is beyond all human conception (human language is singularly deficient in words that describe smell and taste; we always refer our sensations to things generally known)[12] it constantly budded into greenish boils with angry red craters, whose jagged edges were of a livid white; and from these issued pus formed of all things known of man - each one distorted, degraded, blasphemed.

Things innocent, things happy, things holy! every one unspeakably defiled, loathsome, sickening! During the vigil of the day following I recognized one group. I saw Italy. First the Italy of the map, a booted leg. But this leg changed rapidly through myriad phases. It was in turn

---

12. *N.f.A.: This is my general complaint, and that of all research students on the one hand and imaginative writers on the other. We can only express a new idea by combining two or more old ideas, or by the use of metaphor; just so any number can be formed from two others. James Hinton had undoubtedly a perfectly crisp, simple, and concise idea of the "fourth dimension of space"; he found the utmost difficult in conveying it to others, even when they were advanced mathematicians. It is (I believe) the greatest factor that militates against human progress that great men assume that they will be understood by others. Even such a master of lucid English as the late Professor Huxley has been so vitally misunderstood that he has been attacked repeatedly for affirming propositions which he specifically denied in the clearest language.*

the leg of every beast and bird, and in every case each leg was suffering with all diseases from leprosy and elephantiasis to scrofula and syphilis. There was also the consciousness that this was inalienably and for ever part of Arthur.

Then Italy itself, in every detail foul. Then I myself, seen as every woman that has ever been, each one with every disease and torture that Nature and man have plotted in their hellish brains, each ended with a death, a death like Arthur's, whose infinite pangs were added to his own, recognized and accepted as his own.

The same with our child that never was. All children of all nations, incredibly aborted, deformed, tortured, torn in pieces, abused by every foulness that the imagination of an arch-devil could devise.

And so for every thought. I realized that the putrefactive changes in the dead man's brain were setting in motion every memory of his, and smearing them with hell's own paint.

I timed one thought: despite its myriad million details, each one clear, vivid and prolonged, it occupied but three seconds of earthly time.

I considered the incalculable array of the thoughts in his well-furnished mind; I saw that thousands of year would not exhaust them.

But, perhaps, when the brain was destroyed beyond recognition of its component parts –

We have always casually assumed that consciousness depends upon a proper flow of blood in the vessels of the brain; we have never stopped to think whether the records might not be excited in some other manner. And yet we know how tumour of the brain begets hallucinations. Consciousness works strangely; the least disturbance of the blood supply, and it goes out like a candle, or else takes monstrous forms.

Here was the overwhelming truth; "in death man lives again, and lives for ever." Yet we might have thought of it; the phantasmagoria of life which throng the mind of a drowning man might have suggested something of the sort to any man with a sympathetic and active imagination.

Worse even than the thoughts themselves was the apprehension of the thoughts ere they arose. Carbuncles, boils, ulcers, cancers, there is no equivalent for these pustules of the bowels of hell, into whose seething convolutions Arthur sank deeper, ever deeper.

The magnitude of this experience is not to be apprehended by the human mind as we know it. I was convinced that an end must come, for me, with the cremation of the body. I was infinitely glad that he had directed this to be done. But for him, end and beginning seemed to have no meaning. Through it all I seemed to hear the real Arthur's thought. "Though all this is I, yet it is only an accident of me; I stand behind it all, immune, eternal."

It must not be supposed that this in any way detracted from the intensity of the suffering. Rather it added to it. To be loathsome is less than to be linked to loathsomeness. To plunge into impurity is to become deadened to disgust. But to do so and yet to remain pure - every vileness adds a pang. Think of Madonna imprisoned in the body of a prostitute, and compelled to acknowledge "This is I," while never losing her abhorrence. Not only immured in hell, but compelled to partake of its sacraments; not only high priest at its agapae, but begetter and manifestor of its cult; a Christ nauseated at the kiss of Judas, and yet aware that the treachery was his own.

VII

As the putrefaction of the brain advanced, the bursting of the pustules occasionally overlapped, with the result that the confusion and exaggeration of madness with all its poignancy was superadded to the the simpler hell. One might have thought that any confusion would have been a welcome relief to a lucidity so appalling; but this was not so. The torture was infused with a shattering sense of alarm.

The images rose up threatening, disappeared only by blasting themselves into the pultaceous coprolite which was, as it were, the main body of the army which composed Arthur. Deeper and deeper as he dropped the phenomena grew constantly in every sense. Now they were a jungle in which the obscurity and terror of the whole gradually overshadowed even the abhorrence due to every part.

The madness of the living is a thing so abominable and fearful as to chill every human heart with horror; it is less than nothing in comparison with the madness of the dead!

A further complication now arose in the destruction irrevocable and complete of that compensating mechanism of the brain, which is the basis of the sense of time. Hideously distorted and deformed as it had been in the derangement of the brain, like a shapeless jelly shooting out, of a sudden, vast, unsuspected tentacles, the destruction of it cut a thousandfold deeper. The sense of consecution itself was destroyed; things sequent appeared as things superposed or concurrent spatially; a new dimension unfolded; a new destruction of all limitation exposed a new and unfathomable abyss.

To all the rest was added the bewilderment and fear which earthly agaraphobia faintly shadows forth; and at the same time the close immurement weighed upon him, since from infinitude there can be no escape.

Add to this the hopelessness of the monotony of the situation. Infinitely as the phenomena were varied, they were yet recognized as essentially the same. All human tasks are lightened by the certainty that they must end. Even our joys would be intolerable were we convinced that they must endure, through irksomeness and disgust, through weariness and satiety, even for ever and for evermore. In this inhuman, this praeterdiabolic inferno was a wearisome repetition, a harping on the same hateful discord, a continuous nagging whose intervals afforded no relief, only a suspense brimming with the anticipation of some fresh terror.

For hours which were to him eternities this stage continued as each cell that held the record of a memory underwent the degenerative changes which awoke it into hyperbromic purulence.

VIII

The minute bacterial corruption now assumed a gross chemistry. The gases of putrefaction forming in the brain and interpenetrating it were represented in his consciousness by the denizens of the pustules becoming formless and impersonal - Arthur had not yet fathomed the abyss.

Creeping, winding, embracing, the Universe enfolded him, violated him with a nameless and intimate contamination, involved his being in a more suffocating terror.

Now and again it drowned that consciousness in a gulf which his thought could not express to me; and indeed the first and least of his torments is utterly beyond human expression.

It was a woe ever expanded, ever intensified, by each vial of wrath. Memory increased, and understanding grew; the imagination had equally got rid of limit.

What this means who can tell? The human mind cannot really appreciate numbers beyond a score or so; it can deal with numbers by ratiocination, it cannot apprehend them by direct impression. It requires a highly trained intelligence to distinguish between fifteen and sixteen matches on a plate without counting them. In death this limitation is entirely removed. Of the infinite content of the Universe every item was separately realized. The brain of Arthur had become equal in power to that attributed by theologians to the Creator; yet of executive power there was no seed. The impotence of man before circumstance was in him magnified indefinitely, yet without loss of detail or of mass. He understood that The Many was The One without losing or fusing the conception of either. He was God, but a God irretrievably damned: a being infinite, yet limited by the nature of things, and that nature solely compact of loathliness.

IX

I have little doubt that the cremation of my husband's body cut short a process which in the normally buried man continues until no trace of organic substance remains.

The first kiss of the furnace awoke an activity so violent and so vivid that all the past paled in its lurid light.

The quenchless agony of the pang is not to be described; if alleviation there were, it was but the exultation of feeling that this was final.

Not only time, but all expansions of time, all monsters of time's womb were to be annihilated; even the ego might hope some end.

The ego is the "worm that dieth not," and existence the "fire that is not quenched." Yet in this universal pyre, in this barathrum of liquid lava, jetted from the volcanoes of the infinite, this "lake of fire that is reserved for the devil and his angels," might not one at last touch bottom? Ah! but time was no more, neither any eidolon thereof!

The shell was consumed; the gases of the body, combined and recombined, flamed off, free from organic form.

Where was Arthur?

His brain, his individuality, his life, were utterly destroyed. As separate things, yes: Arthur had entered the universal consciousness.

And I heard this utterance: or rather this is my translation into English of a single thought whose synthesis is "Woe."

Substance is called spirit or matter.

Spirit and matter are one, indivisible, eternal, indestructible.

Infinite and eternal change!

Infinite and eternal pain!

No absolute: no truth, no beauty, no idea, nothing but the whirlwinds of form, unresting, unappeasable.

Eternal hunger! Eternal war! Change and pain infinite and unceasing.

There is no individuality but in illusion. And the illusion is change and pain, and its destruction is change and pain, and its new segregation from the infinite and eternal is change and pain; and substance infinite and eternal is change and pain unspeakable.

Beyond thought, which is change and pain, lies being, which is change and pain.

These were the last words intelligible; they lapsed into the eternal moan, Woe! Woe! Woe! Woe! Woe! Woe! Woe! in unceasing monotony that rings always in my ears if I let my thought fall from the height of activity, listen to the voice of my sensorium.

In my sleep I am partially protected, and I keep a lamp constantly alight to burn tobacco in the room: but yet too often my dreams throb with that reiterated Woe! Woe! Woe! Woe! Woe! Woe! Woe!

X

The final stage is clearly enough inevitable, unless we believe the Buddhist theories, which I am somewhat inclined to do, as their theory of the Universe is precisely confirmed in every detail by the facts here set down. But it is one thing to recognize a disease, another to discover a remedy. Frankly, my whole being revolts from their methods, and I had rather acquiesce in the ultimate destiny and achieve it as quickly as may be. My earnest preoccupation is to avoid the preliminary tortures, and I am convinced that the explosion of a dynamite cartridge in the mouth is the most practicable method of effecting this. There is just the possibility that if all thinking minds, all "spiritual beings," were thus destroyed, and especially if all organic life could be annihilated, that the Universe might cease to be, since (as Bishop Berkeley has shown) it can only exist in some thinking mind. And there is really no evidence (in spite of Berkeley) for the existence of any extra-human consciousness. Matter in itself may think, in a sense, but its monotony of woe is less awful than its abomination, the building up of high and holy things only to drag them through infamy and terror to the old abyss.

I shall consequently cause this record to be widely distributed. The note-books of my work with Arthur (Vols, I-CCXIV) will be edited by Professor von Buehle, whose marvellous mind may perhaps discover some escape from the destiny which menaces mankind. Everything is in order in these note-books; and I am free to die, for I can endure no more, and above all things I dread the onset of illness, and the possibility of natural or accidental death.

Note

I am glad to have the opportunity of publishing, in a journal so widely read by the profession, the MS. of the widow of the late Professor Blair.

Her mind undoubtedly became unhinged through grief at her husband's death; the medical man who attended him in his last illness grew alarmed at her condition, and had her watched. She tried (fruitlessly) to purchase dynamite at several shops, but on her going to the laboratory of her late husband, and attempting to manufacture Chloride of Nitrogen, obviously for the purpose of suicide, she was seized, certified insane, and placed in my care.

The case is most unusual in several respects.

(1) I have never known her inaccurate in any statement of veritable fact.

(2) She can undoubtedly read thoughts in an astonishing manner. In particular, she is

actually useful to me by her ability to foretell attacks of acute insanity in my patients. Some hours before they occur she can predict them to a minute. On an early occasion my disbelief in her power led to the dangerous wounding of one of my attendants.

(3) She combines a fixed determination of suicide (in the extraordinary manner described by her) with an intense fear of death. She smokes uninterruptedly, and I am obliged to allow her to fumigate her room at night with the same drug.

(4) She is certainly only twenty-four years old, and any competent judge would with equal certainty declare her sixty.

(5) Professor von Buehle, to whom the note-books were {173} sent, addressed to me a long and urgent telegram, begging her release on condition that she would promise not to commit suicide, but go to work with him in Bonn. I have yet to learn, however, that German professors, however eminent, have any voice in

the management of a private asylum in England, and I am certain that the Lunacy Commissioners will uphold me in my refusal to consider the question.

It will then be clearly understood that this document is published with all reserve as the lucubration of a very peculiar, perhaps unique, type of insanity.

V. English, M.D.

V. ENGLISH, M.D.

THE TESTAMENT
OF MAGDALEN
BLAIR
The End

AFTERWORD

By Giancarlo D'Anello

Few 20th century people have been able to move through such different circles as Aleister Crowley. Writer, poet, editor, magician, reviewer, climber, novelist, painter, the boy born in 1875 in the small village of Royal Leamington Spa, located in central England, more precisely in the county of Warwickshire, influenced many people, being a central figure for several generations of musicians, writers, artists and esotericists. The Brazilian rocker Raul Seixas was one of them.

Raul Seixas has already stated that his album “Novo Aeon”, released in 1975, was entirely inspired by the “Book of the Law” (Liber AL vel Legis). This album also was composed in partnership with Marcelo Motta, who was a member of occult groups, founder of the Thelemic Brazilian circle “Sociedade Novo Aeon” and instructor of Paulo Coelho at the Ordo Templis Orientis, another esoteric group that also had Aleister Crowley as a member at its British headquarters. The song "Sociedade Alternativa" (Alternative Society) itself was inspired by a booklet called "Liber OZ", which Crowley wrote in 1941.

Jimmy Page, the founder and leader of Led Zeppelin, was also deeply influenced by the man of Royal Leamington Spa, and used the same Crowleyan phrase that Raul Seixas used - “Do what thou wilt” - to record the album "Led Zeppelin III", released in 1970. In addition to be a student of the Thelema religion, Page was also a passionate collector of the English magician's memorabilia. So much that he bought in the 70’s the Boleskine House, a Scottish country house that once belonged to Crowley.

Like Seixas and Page, we can remember hundreds of other popular culture references to Crowley, such as his appearance on the cover of the Beatles most celebrated album - Sgt. Pepper's Lonely Hearts Club Band -, he is also mentioned in the song "Quicksand", by David Bowie, in the classic "Mr. Crowley ", by Ozzy Osbourne, on the album"Chemical Wedding", by Bruce Dickinson, among many others. His influence went far beyond his writings because his enigmatic, strange and controversial figure took higher and more perennial flights in the cultural imagination of the West than his own ideas. For the past 70 years, the world seemed to be more interested in the character than in the writer. Many have heard of him, but few took a serious look over his writings; even less are those who sought to understand his fictional works, which directly or indirectly give clues about his beliefs and esoteric methodology.

"The Testament of Magdalen Blair" first appeared in the 1913 edition of The Equinox magazine. This magazine, which was founded by Crowley in 1903 and continued to be published until 1998, used to publish texts on various topics such as the occult, poetry, biographies, short stories, works of art and mystical reflections. Crowley released there a lot of prose and poetry material that was previously rejected by other publishers due to his bad reputation. During the years that he published in it, he had great freedom of expression, and could expose a creative side that was not so well known by his peers and colleagues.

This tale, which express the most ferocious cosmic horror, preceded Lovecraft's writings, and helped to consolidate - in the underground of literature - this subgenre that throughout the 20th century would be consecrated by Robert Bloch, Clark Ashton Smith, Thomas Ligotti and, of course, by the Providence's master. The echoes that influenced the writing of this tale can also be traced in the texts of Arthur Machen, Algernon Blackwood and, mainly, in the short story "The Facts That Involved the Case of Mr. Valdemar", by Edgar Allan Poe, which has a very similar premise.

Despite the atrocious existential pessimism that the tale expresses, "The Testament of Magdalen Blair" has a strong Buddhist component in its thesis. Its theme was, as stated by Crowley himself at the time of the republication of the story in 1929, suggested by Charles Henry Allan Bennett, who was a great promoter of Buddhist ideas in the West and also a colleague of Crowley in the Hermetic Order of the Golden Dawn.

However, regardless of the reader's ideas about spirituality, what is at hand is a horrifying story, a forgotten horror classic that expresses in the cruelest form what, according to Lovecraft, was the man's oldest and most primitive emotion. An extreme imaginative exercise about the hidden realities and the nature of eternity.

Despite the bad reputation that his name still has today, retrieving Aleister Crowley's fictional writing is important to understand how the myth was built around him, and how lost pearls of speculative fiction can help us to understand the chasms of imagination that man is capable to build.

www.ingramcontent.com/pod-product-compliance
Lightning Source LLC
Chambersburg PA
CBHW030601310726
48979CB00003B/528

9781838047306